D0589870

BUS

Please renew or return items by the date shown on your receipt

www.hertsdirect.org/libraries

Renewals and enquiries: 0300 123 4049

Textphone for hearing or speech impaired 0300 123 4041

Hertfordshire

A Note from the Author

I love a good zombie film.

I love a *bad* zombie film too. I love any kind of zombie film. As long as it's gory and nasty, I'm happy. In fact, the nastier and gorier it is, the better.

No wonder I've always wanted to write a zombie story myself. But in my case, I felt like doing something different. I didn't want to write about un-dead monsters who feed on the brains of their victims. I thought it would be interesting if *my* zombies weren't the bad guys. If they were in fact the heroes.

That's how *Dead Brigade* came about.

The zombies in this book may be rotten. But they're not rotten to the core!

This book is dedicated to all the political leaders who choose peace instead of war. If they exist.

Contents

Chapter 1

Kurdistan

A thin wind slid like a ghost between the mountain peaks. Sleet seeped down from a grey sky. The cold wet flakes pattered into the soldiers' faces, making their eyes sting. The silence all around was vast. That silence must have existed millions of years ago, before the human race appeared. Every footstep the soldiers made sounded as loud as a shout.

There were nine of them in the patrol. They had been in the Zagros mountains for nearly a week. They had trudged along narrow, stony paths. They had scrambled up steep, rough slopes. They had camped out in the open, shivering in sleeping-bags that never felt quite thick enough to keep out the cold. The SA80 rifles and Bergen packs they had to carry seemed to weigh a ton. Their bellies rumbled, because army rations never quite filled them up.

The soldiers felt as though they had been tramping through the mountains for months, not days. They had not yet seen any sign of the men they were hunting. They were starting to wonder if the men even existed. The only living beings the soldiers had seen, apart from each other, were a few wild goats. Once, they'd heard the cry of an eagle. They had looked up, but the bird had been hidden in the clouds. That cry was the most lonely sound in the world.

Now the patrol's leader, Captain Carr, ordered the men to take a rest. The soldiers dropped their Bergens and sat on them. They brewed some tea and shared out chocolate and cigarettes.

Carr drew Sergeant Dex Hammond aside for a quiet word.

"What's your view on this, sergeant?" Carr asked Hammond. "Wild goose chase or what?"

"The intelligence was pretty clear, sir," Hammond replied. He was Carr's second-in-command on this mission. "The rebels are holed up somewhere round here."

"Yes, but what do *you* think?" Carr said.

Hammond paused. "Satellite hasn't spotted anyone. But the rebels are locals. They know this region like the back of their hands. They know every nook and cranny. If they want to hide here, then they won't be seen. Not by satellites and most of all not by us. I expect they can hear us coming a mile off."

"You think we haven't a hope of finding them," said Carr.

"I'd say the chances were somewhere between slim and nil," said Hammond.

Carr gave a quick grin. "I've always admired you for being so frank, Hammond. And you're right. There's a saying in these parts. *The Kurds have no friends but the mountains.* And it's true. The mountains have always been a safe hiding place for them, most of all up here in the north. However ..."

Carr gave a shrug.

"We don't have much choice," he went on. "We have to keep looking. These rebels have become a right pain in the neck. The Kurds didn't even have a proper country until a few years ago, when Iraq was liberated. Now that they do, the rebels are trying hard to make it an Islamic state."

"But our leaders don't like that idea," said Hammond.

"The West wants a democratic Kurdistan, yes. One where the people choose their rulers, rather than God doing it."

"Because of all that uranium that's been found down in the south. Europe and America are keen to get their hands on it. That won't happen if Kurdistan goes Islamic."

The rebels were attacking anyone from the West, not just the troops, all across Kurdistan. They shot people from the mining companies, who were working on ways of getting the uranium out of the ground. They lobbed mortars into the British and American embassies. There had been suicide bombings in several towns and cities, including the new Kurdish capital, the city of Van. The Independent Republic of Kurdistan was in chaos, and British troops had been called in to help keep the peace. And to wipe out the rebels.

"We're soldiers, sergeant," said Captain Carr. "It's not up to us to ask why we have to do something. We just do it. So come on. Let's get going again."

He ordered the men to get back on their feet. The patrol marched onward.

An hour passed, and Hammond began to feel uneasy. The silence had grown deeper. The wind had dropped. The sleet still fell, like icy needles, but it was as though the mountains were holding their breath. Waiting for something to happen.

Hammond told himself that it was just because he was tired. His brain was fuzzy after a week without a proper night's sleep. He was starting to see things that weren't there.

But still he couldn't shake off the feeling that someone was watching the patrol.

He seemed to sense eyes peering down from the crags above. Someone was following the patrol's progress. Someone knew the soldiers were there, and was lying in wait for them.

Hammond should have said something about this to Captain Carr, but he knew what would happen if he did. Carr would laugh at him and tell him not to be foolish. The boss wasn't the kind of man who paid much attention to "funny feelings". He put his faith in things he could feel and touch. In that respect he was typical of anyone who had trained at Sandhurst. There, at the Royal Military Academy, they turned out officers who did everything by the book. But Hammond thought they also turned out officers who didn't have any common sense, or any instinct for danger.

Unless Hammond could prove that there was someone up there watching, Carr would never believe him. And Hammond couldn't prove it. He wasn't even 100 per cent sure of it himself. He only had his gut to go on, and his gut was telling him that the rebels were hiding close by. The patrol was going to engage with the enemy very soon.

He gripped his rifle hard.

The soldiers reached the top of a sharp ridge. At their feet lay a long, V-shaped valley. Carr told one of the men, Private Andrews, to check their position with his GPS unit.

Andrews looked at the screen of his little hand-held device. He said, "Yep, I've managed to pinpoint where we are. If this is right, we're in the middle of fucking nowhere."

The others chuckled. Their laughter rolled down into the valley, with an echo like faint thunder.

"That's enough of that," said Carr, with a flicker of a smile. "Send a note of our position back to base. Then we head down that way." He pointed towards the bottom of the valley.

Hammond looked. It was very narrow down there. The steep sides of the valley were studded with rocks and thorny trees. The rocks were large enough for men to hide behind. The trees too.

"Sir, I'm not sure that's such a good idea," Hammond said to Carr.

Carr frowned. "What do you mean?"

"If you'll excuse me, the bottom of that valley is the perfect spot for an ambush. We should avoid it and go around the top."

"I hear what you say, Sergeant Hammond," said Carr. "However, down through the valley is the fastest route, not to mention the simplest. If we go around the top, it'll mean going an extra three or four kilometres."

"But sir, the extra distance doesn't matter," said Hammond. "It's not as if we're in a hurry to get somewhere. This is a search mission, not a race."

"True," said Carr. "So let's search through the valley. That's an order."

"But, sir – "

"That's an order," said Carr again.

Hammond bit his lip. There was no point arguing. The boss had made up his mind. They would just have to live with it.

The patrol set off down into the valley, single file.

Hammond switched his SA80 from "safety" to triple-shot mode. Fear prickled through his body. He prayed that he was wrong. He prayed that his feeling of being watched was all in his mind.

But he couldn't help picturing the rebels in his mind. They were lying silent and still among the rocks and trees. They had AK-47s in their hands and the British soldiers in their sights. He saw their dusty, drab clothes and turbans, perfect cover in this kind of country. These were men who could merge with the mountains they lived in, vanishing into the landscape.

A bead of sweat trickled down his spine.

Then something exploded twenty metres away. A rocket-propelled grenade. It kicked up a shower of dirt and stone.

The patrol threw themselves to the ground, flat on their faces.

Bullets thwipped and bounced all around them.

Captain Carr shouted, "Engage! Engage! Return fire!"

The SA80s barked.

Another RPG landed, and someone screamed.

Hammond saw Private Andrews. Andrews was thrashing around on the ground. Half his face had been torn away. Blood poured from the ragged hole where his left eye should have been. Beside him another of the men

was lying dead. His belly had burst open.
A mass of mangled guts spilled out from
the hole.

The SA80 leapt in Hammond's hands as he
squeezed the trigger. He strafed the sides of
the valley with bursts of gunfire. He couldn't
see the enemy's positions. He shot without
aiming. It felt as if he was fighting the
landscape itself.

The valley rumbled with the echo of the
guns. The sleet was still falling, slow and
white and steady. Above, the sky was a blank
slate of grey.

The sounds faded into nothing. Hammond
could no longer hear anything, not the
soldiers screaming, not the rattle of gunfire.

It was like a dream.

It *was* a dream.

Hammond snapped awake. He was in bed.
He was at home, in his flat in the mess. His

radio alarm clock said 3:14 AM. The numbers glowed red in the dark.

His heart was pounding. His skin was damp with sweat.

Hammond staggered to the bathroom and soaked his face in cold water. He went into the living room, which had a small kitchen, and made himself coffee. Then he turned on the TV and clicked it to the Discovery Channel. He knew that he wouldn't get back to sleep tonight. He never did when he had this dream. He watched a series of films about sharks for the rest of the night, until dawn broke.

Then he put on his kit and went to work.

Chapter 2

Quarter-master

Since the events in Kurdistan six years earlier, Sergeant Dex Hammond had not seen active duty. He still served with his regiment, but he now had a job in the quarter-master's office. He sat at a desk and placed orders for food, uniforms and weapons. Requests came in either by phone or email. Hammond had to deal with them. He worked closely with the barracks catering staff and the RQMS, the regimental quarter-master.

Sometimes he had to travel to meet with a supplier. Most often it would be someone from a wholesale food company. But this didn't happen often.

Hammond hardly ever left the barracks any more. This was his home, his life. His parents were dead. He had no brothers or sisters. He didn't have a girlfriend. He had nowhere to go. The room where he spent his days was tiny, not much bigger than a coffin. This was what was left of an army career that had once been bright and hopeful.

This morning, Hammond sat at his computer, staring blankly at the screen. He yawned. His eyes were red-rimmed and bloodshot. The dream kept coming back to him in vivid flashes. The Zagros mountains. The valley. The rebels' attack. He knew he would never be free of the memories of what had happened. Dr Kline, the regiment's counsellor, kept telling him the memories would fade in the end. The dreams would stop coming. He said Hammond just had to give it time.

But what did Dr Kline know? Had Dr Kline ever been under fire? No. Had Dr Kline ever seen men he knew, friends, get ripped to shreds right before his very eyes? No. Had Dr Kline ever heard the sound of bullets thudding into flesh, or heard grown men weeping like children as they died, crying out for their mothers? No.

Dr Kline couldn't possibly understand what it was like. That day in Kurdistan was carved in Hammond's head like words on a gravestone. During the daytime he could shut the memories out. If he stayed busy, they wouldn't come to the front of his mind. But, asleep, he could do nothing about the dreams. The nightmares. If he was still having nightmares about Kurdistan six years after it happened, then he was going to be having those nightmares for the rest of his life.

The phone rang.

"Quarter-master's office. Hammond speaking."

"Sergeant Hammond?"

He knew the voice, but it took Hammond a moment or two to place it. Then he remembered. He had heard that voice just last night, in his sleep.

"Captain Carr," he said.

"It's Major Carr now," said Carr.

"Sorry, sir," said Hammond. In truth, he wasn't too bothered that he had got Carr's rank wrong.

"That's all right, sergeant," said Carr. "No reason why you should know that I'd been promoted. After all, it's been – what? Five years?"

"Six," said Hammond.

"Yes. Six years since that nasty business in the Zagros mountains."

Nasty business? Hammond felt a sizzle of anger. Was that all Carr thought it was? A nasty business? Carr's attitude had cost seven men their lives. And now he was remembering it as if it was just some bad holiday he'd been on ...

Was that how little Carr cared about what he'd done?

With a huge effort, Hammond kept calm.

"How may I help you, sir?" he asked.

"As a matter of fact," Carr replied, "I think there's something I can do to help you. What are you up to at the moment? Not too busy?"

Hammond looked at his computer screen. Nothing on his to-do list had to be done right now.

"I think I can clear space for you," he said.

"Good," said Carr. "I'm down on the square, talking to you from my mobile. See you in five minutes."

Carr hung up without a goodbye.

Hammond sat for a while, thinking. Carr was here, at the barracks? He'd come all this way just to see Hammond? He'd popped back into Hammond's life, right out of the blue? Why? What for?

Well, there was only one way to find out.

Hammond got up, put on his beret, and strode outside.

Chapter 3

Major Carr's Offer

Out on the parade square, a few cadets were doing drill. A sergeant major yelled at them like the top of his head was going to explode. The cadets cringed from the noise he made. They looked so small and puny. *Was I like that once?* Hammond thought.

Hammond had been eighteen when he'd joined the Army. He'd wanted to be a soldier for as long as he could remember. For a boy from a run-down London council estate, joining the army had been one of the few worth-while choices he could make. It was better than hanging out on the streets and getting into drugs and all that gangsta-hoodie bollocks, which was what most of Hammond's mates ended up doing. That kind of lifestyle had no prospects in it at all. The army promised Hammond some kind of future, a way forward. A way out.

But also, Hammond had really wanted to serve his country. He'd wanted to be useful and make a difference. He'd believed he would be able to do that by becoming a soldier.

He believed it still, even though for the past six years his life in the army had been nothing but guilt and shame.

Hammond looked around for Major Carr. He saw a stout man standing at the edge of the square, looking smart and splendid in dress uniform.

The man waved at Hammond. At first Hammond couldn't believe it was Major Carr. He had become very fat since Hammond had last seen him. In fact, he was obese.

Hammond walked over to him. He remembered how Carr had looked six years ago. Then, Carr had been tall and stocky, built like a rugby player. He hadn't been slim by any means, but he'd not been carrying the huge bulk that he did now. Carr must be at least 70 kilos heavier than before. A second chin now hung below his first. His cheeks were puffy, making his eyes look pinched and small. His fingers had become chubby, like pink slugs.

Hammond felt proud of himself. He went jogging every day and worked out at the gym, keeping his body in trim. Carr, on the other hand, seemed to have done nothing in the past six years but eat.

He saluted Carr. Carr saluted back.

"Nice to see you again, sergeant," said Carr. "You're looking in good shape."

Hammond felt like saying, *You aren't*. But he just nodded and said, "Thanks."

"Care to take a stroll with me?" Carr asked.

They walked away from the parade square, side by side. It was a crisp autumn morning. The sun shone, the trees were golden, and rooks cawed. The air was chilly but not cold. Hammond's and Carr's breath came out in fine, smoky coils.

"Yes, you're looking in good shape," Carr said after they had gone 100 metres in silence, "but you look rather tired too. It shows around your eyes. They've got bags under them. You look like you haven't slept well in ages."

"I haven't."

"I know," said Carr. "I've read a recent psych report about you. Bad dreams, is that what's wrong?"

"Something like that," said Hammond. *Why would Carr want to see one of Dr Kline's reports about me?* he thought. *Why is Carr interested in me, suddenly, after we haven't seen each other for so long?*

Hammond tried to think what Carr's job was in the army these days. Carr had left the regiment, and Hammond had heard it said that he was involved in special ops – secret missions, that sort of thing. If so, it must be in an admin role. Nobody as fat as he was could be in active service.

"It's Kurdistan, isn't it?" said Carr. "You still can't get over what happened there. You're still carrying the bad memories around with you. But I don't see why. I don't understand how that's such a problem for you. We survived, didn't we? You and I. We held out, just the two of us, for the best part of an hour. It was a near thing for a while, I admit. I thought our ammo was going to run out. But we got a distress call out on the radio. Chopper came, the rebels ran off, and we were air-lifted out of there. We lived. You can't really ask for more than that, can you?"

"We lived, sir, yes," said Hammond. "But seven other men didn't."

Carr shrugged. "That's just how it goes. Luck of the draw. Some make it, some don't. That's war. It's nothing to feel bad about. What happened happened, sergeant. You can't keep carrying it around inside you like some sort of – of hot coal. Otherwise it'll burn you up and destroy you."

"I can't just forget about it, sir," Hammond said. "If we hadn't gone into that valley – "

Carr stopped Hammond before he could go on. He held up a hand.

"Not again," he said with a sigh. "Let's not go over all this again. It was sorted out later at the enquiry. Three senior officers of this regiment agreed that nobody was to blame. Our patrol was the victim of a surprise attack, that's it. The rebels got the drop on us. It couldn't be helped."

"They wouldn't have pinned us down like that if we'd done as I suggested," said Hammond. "We should have gone around the valley, not up it. That way they'd never have trapped us in a cross-fire."

"A point which you made very clear at the enquiry," said Carr. His tone was still warm but there was a hint of frost in it. "Several times. At the top of your voice. You kicked up a hell of a fuss, sergeant. You made quite a scene, with all that shouting and finger-pointing you did. And where did it get you?

Nowhere. Have you ever thought about why you do the job you do? Why you spend every day counting flak jackets and meat pies?"

Hammond didn't answer. He knew the reason as well as Carr did.

"It's because you made trouble," Carr said. "You rocked the boat. And if there's one thing the army hates and cannot forgive, it's people rocking the boat. You kept insisting someone must have done something wrong. But how could that be? They gave us medals, didn't they? Distinguished service medals for bravery under fire. Both of us. How could someone have done anything wrong if they gave us medals?"

Hammond looked at the rows of bright ribbons on the front of Carr's tunic. There were plenty of them. Hammond's view was that the medals could only be for sucking up. In that case the ribbons ought to be brown, to match the colour of Carr's nose, which

27

was stuck firmly up the backsides of the top brass.

Hammond had turned down his medal. He would have felt ashamed to wear it.

"Anyway," Carr went on, "I didn't come here so that we could rake up any of this old, old business. It's water under the bridge as far as I'm concerned."

"Why *are* you here, sir?" Hammond asked.

"I have a little job for you, Sergeant Hammond." Carr stopped, turned and fixed him with an even gaze. "An odd sort of job. A one-off, in fact."

Hammond was quite eager to hear what it was. He tried not to let this show, but something in his face must have given him away. A job. Could this be active duty of some kind? At last?

"Ah, that's got your interest, hasn't it?" said Carr. "I thought it might. This job is the sort of thing that could well get your career back on track. Do it well, and there's a chance you can put Kurdistan behind you for good and start to move on again."

"Why me, sir?" said Hammond. He still did not trust Carr. "Why are you offering this job, any job, to me?"

Carr smiled. His eyes grew narrow and his cheeks bulged. He looked like a cat that had just gulped down a plump, tasty mouse.

"First of all, I think you deserve it," he said. "Second, I think it'll suit you. We're looking for a man who could do a rather special thing for us. You came into my mind at once."

Carr moved closer to Hammond and spoke in a low voice.

"But the third reason I'm offering it to you," Carr said, "is because you don't really have a choice. You're not going to say no.

It's this or staying a no-hoper for the rest of your life. So you can tell me right now if you're not interested. But if that's the case, then you'll remain a sergeant till you retire. Is that what you want?"

Chapter 4

Project Osiris

Three days later, Hammond was at Wild Hare Park in Berkshire. This was one of the Ministry of Defence's top-secret research and development centres. Here, scientists dreamed up all sorts of new weapons and tested them.

It was a dull-looking place, from the outside. Wild Hare Park was enclosed by a high fence. Inside this fence there were several brick and concrete buildings. None of the buildings was more than two storeys tall. Around them spread rolling lawns dotted with trees. From a distance Wild Hare Park looked almost like a modern school.

That was because most of what happened at Wild Hare Park went on underground. Beneath the buildings lay a basement complex, floor upon floor dug deep into the earth. It was known as the Vault. Here, there were labs and machine shops. There were warehouses full of state-of-the-art armaments. There were bio-hazard chambers where scientists cooked up deadly germs and chemicals.

Hammond travelled down into the Vault in a lift. With him went two royal military policemen, who were armed with handguns. The RMPs wouldn't talk to Hammond. Their job was to stay with him wherever he went. Security at Wild Hare Park was very tight. It had taken three days for Hammond to get a permit to visit the place. The RMPs had orders to shoot him at once if he stepped even a millimetre out of line.

Five floors down, the lift stopped.

The door slid open and Hammond was greeted by a middle-aged woman with thick glasses and glossy, dark grey hair. She kept her hair tied back in a tight bun, and it shone like polished iron. Her name was Professor Ruth Lessing.

"Welcome to the Vault, Sergeant Hammond," Professor Lessing said. "I hope you'll enjoy working with us."

"Hold on," said Hammond. "I haven't agreed to work with you yet."

Professor Lessing looked confused. "Oh. I thought this was a done deal. That you'd accepted the job."

Hammond chose his words with care. "I told Major Carr I'd do it but only if I felt it was something I could do well. I've no idea what the job involves. No one's told me anything about anything. I'm in the dark."

"Then I shall do what I can to explain things to you," said Professor Lessing. She rounded up her little group. "Come along, then. This way."

Professor Lessing led Hammond along a maze of well-lit corridors. The two RMPs followed like shadows. People in lab coats swished past. Some of them said hello to Professor Lessing, others seemed too lost in thought to notice her or anyone else. Hammond walked by endless doors. One or two were open and he got a glimpse of the rooms inside them.

In one room he saw someone wearing a bio-hazard suit, ready to enter a sealed chamber. The suit covered the person from head to toe in white plastic, making him (or her) look alien and unreal, like a ghost from another world.

In another room there were animals in cages – mostly mice and small monkeys, but cats and dogs too. The cages were behind a glass screen, but all the animals were very restless. The monkeys most of all were jumping around and howling. Hammond could hear the panic in their cries, even through the glass.

They arrived at a steel door marked **Project Osiris**. Professor Lessing unlocked the door by tapping a code number into a key-pad on the wall.

Beyond, there was another steel door. It wouldn't open until the first steel door was closed and locked.

"We have to take great care," said Professor Lessing.

Hammond clenched his teeth together. What was he getting himself into? He'd had a bad feeling about this whole business, ever since Major Carr had told him that the job was at Wild Hare Park. People told strange tales about this place. The scientists here got up to all kinds of weird and dangerous stuff.

Hammond remembered that, 50 years ago, some soldiers had been exposed to atomic radiation at Wild Hare Park. It had been part of an experiment to see how the radiation affected the human body. Almost all of the soldiers had died of cancer within a year. Hammond shivered to think that people could do such a thing to their fellow men, all in the name of scientific research.

He shivered also as he thought about the name Project Osiris. It sounded sinister. What did it mean? Osiris was some old god from Egypt, wasn't he? But Hammond didn't know any more about him than that.

The room on the other side of the second door was dimly lit. The air felt chilly and dry.

"We have to keep the room cool," Professor Lessing explained. "It slows the rate of decay."

Hammond didn't understand. "The rate of decay?"

"Let me start with first things first," said Professor Lessing. "Tell me what you see."

Hammond peered into the room. His eyes took a few seconds to adjust to the low lighting. As they did, he became aware of a faint smell. It reminded him of seaweed, for some reason. The smell of seaweed on a pebble beach, sour and rotting.

In the room there were ten steel beds, lined up in two rows of five. The beds were made of metal and didn't have mattresses. They were similar to the slabs for dead bodies in a hospital morgue.

On each bed a figure lay on its back. They were men, naked, lying quite still, with their hands by their sides. At their heads were computer screens, softly glowing. The screens displayed numbers and graphs, and were changing all the time, showing fresh readings.

"They're ... asleep?" said Hammond. The men didn't look to him as if they were asleep, but he couldn't think of any other reason for them to be lying there.

"Why don't you take a closer look?" said Professor Lessing.

Hammond did not trust her tone. Professor Lessing sounded like a stage magician who was about to play a trick on someone from the audience. There was a hint of a giggle in her voice.

Hammond went up to the nearest bed. He leaned over and looked closely at the man lying on it.

The man was dead.

He was a corpse.

His eyes were closed. His face was blue-grey, as was the rest of his body. His lips were parted, showing his long yellow teeth. His skin was withered and flakes of it had peeled off here and there. The flesh beneath was the colour of cooked liver.

Hammond had just enough time to wonder why Professor Lessing was keeping dead bodies in a room like this.

Then the corpse's eyes flicked open and he reached up and grabbed Hammond.

Chapter 5
The Next Best Thing to Life

Hammond yelped in shock.

The dead man's grip was cold and dry. He was holding Hammond's wrist so hard that it hurt. Hammond tried shaking the dead man's hand off, but the corpse wouldn't let go.

The dead man stared up at him. The whites of his eyes were zig-zagged with tiny black squiggles. The coloured parts of the eyes were so pale, they were almost white.

A horrible moan emerged from the dead man's mouth. It was like the sound of a wind moving through the branches of trees in winter. It was a hiss and a crackle and a sigh.

At last Hammond managed to prise off the corpse's fingers.

The dead man's hand sank down onto the bed. He stopped moaning. His eyes fluttered shut.

Hammond staggered away from the bed. He spun round angrily.

"What the hell is this?" he shouted at Professor Lessing. "That thing is dead! I know what a dead body looks like, and that's one. How come it can move? What in God's name are you up to here?"

"Calm down, Sergeant Hammond," said Professor Lessing. She gave a small smile. "No need to get worked up. You're quite right. The fellow on that bed is dead. Him and the other nine. All quite dead."

"But – "

"Why don't we go somewhere else?" Professor Lessing suggested. "My study, perhaps. I have some brandy there, and you look as if you could do with a good stiff drink."

As they left the chilly room, Hammond couldn't help taking a quick glance over his shoulder. All ten bodies were lying still.

Thank God.

Moments later, Hammond was sitting with a glass of brandy in his hand. Professor Lessing was perched on a desk that was stacked high with folders, documents and science journals. The RMPs were by the door. Their faces were like masks, but Hammond had the feeling they were rather amused. They had found his moment of fright with the corpse funny. Perhaps they had been expecting something like that would happen.

The study was small and cramped. There were no windows, so the air was stuffy. Drawings of the human body hung on the walls. One of them showed all the muscles and tendons, another the skeleton, a third the veins and the nervous system. Metal shelves were stacked with items of electronic equipment. Slivers of green circuit board were packed close to reels of insulated wire. Micro-chips lay in a small pile like a nest of silicon spiders. The hard drive of a computer sat, half pulled to pieces, as though it had been dissected.

The brandy began to take effect. Hammond's heart rate began to return to normal. He was getting over his shock.

"You see, Project Osiris is all about new recruits," Professor Lessing explained. "Or rather, the lack of new recruits. The army is in real trouble. It's having a hard time finding new troops to replace the ones who've died or retired. Recruitment levels are at an all-time low. You know this as well as I do, Sergeant Hammond. Most likely even better than I do. And why is the army having such a problem?"

It was as if Professor Lessing was giving a lecture. She replied to her own question.

"Because the world has changed," she said. "War isn't about nation against nation any more. It's about dealing with terrorism. It's about stopping small bands of outcasts and rebels from bombing and killing. There's none of that 'laying down your life for your country' stuff any more. That means nothing these days. Soldiers have become a kind of armed police, going wherever there's trouble."

Hammond nodded. Professor Lessing was right. Very few people wanted to be soldiers these days. The number of troops who were fit for service was dropping year by year, and that wasn't just because the pay was awful. No one saw army life as noble, the way they used to in the past. The time for great land battles was over. It was hard to take pride in shabby little conflicts against bands of non-army men and women with guns and bombs and a hatred of the system.

Hammond knew this all too well. He himself had been taken in by the dream of comradeship and military glory. It was simply not true. Yet he still clung to it, even now.

"So," Professor Lessing went on, "here at Wild Hare Park we were given the task of finding a new source of recruits. My field of interest has always been ways of improving the human body. For years I've done research into how to make the body's reflexes work better. The means I use are not natural ones. I've been trying to create a better soldier, one who's stronger and faster than a normal person. What I came up with was a system that uses electrical impulses to speed up the muscles and nerves. But to begin with, I just couldn't get it to work. When I tried it out on animals they went mad and died."

Professor Lessing shrugged.

"This was a setback, of course," she said. "Then I had a stroke of genius. What if I carried out my work on dead animals instead of living ones? My first idea failed because the animals' bodies couldn't cope with the extra energy being put through them. It was too much for their systems. Their brains fried and their hearts gave out. But the same thing wouldn't happen, I thought, if they weren't alive to begin with. And that's how Project Osiris got started. I named it after the Egyptian god of death. Although, in fact, Osiris isn't just the god of death, he's also the god of life and rebirth."

So that was it. Hammond found his voice at last. "You can bring the dead back to life," he said in a husky croak. "You did it on animals and now you can do it on people. Is that it?"

"No," said Professor Lessing. "It looks that way, but no. What I do to these corpses makes them look as if they were alive. There are battery packs wired into their heads. When you went in there you couldn't see them. The packs are attached to the corpses' backs. The batteries send a charge through the brains and into the nerves. It isn't as simple as it sounds. The timing and level of the charge must be finely tuned. It's taken me ages to get right. Also, I had to invent a new kind of blood. Have you ever heard of nanobots?"

"No," said Hammond.

"They're tiny machines," said Professor Lessing. "So small you can't even see them with a microscope. Not much bigger than atoms. The blood I devised contains trillions of nanobots. They help conduct the electrical charge around the dead men's bodies. In effect the blood is a kind of 'liquid computer' inside the corpses."

She broke off.

"But I can tell this sort of stuff isn't as absorbing to you as it is to me," she said. "Your eyes have glazed over."

"Sorry," said Hammond. "I'm not much of a scientist."

"Fair enough," said Professor Lessing. "The details don't matter anyway. The result is what matters. And the result here is that I can make those dead men stand up, walk, raise their arms – maybe even dance! It isn't life," Professor Lessing concluded. "But it's the next best thing."

"What's my part in all of this?" Hammond said. "What am I here to do?"

"Oh, that's very simple, sergeant," said Professor Lessing. "What you have to do is take those ten corpses and train them. You're here to turn them into soldiers."

Chapter 6

Perfect Soldiers

It was a test of nerves.

Hammond stood in a large underground bunker, one of the Vault's many shooting ranges. The room was empty now. The targets and firing posts had been removed. Neon strip-lights buzzed overhead. Their glow flickered on the bunker's rough, bare concrete walls.

Men in white plastic suits were rolling trolleys in through the entrance, one by one.

The corpses lay on the trolleys. It was the second time Hammond had seen the dead men, and they weren't naked this time. They had been dressed in olive-green uniforms. There were boots on their feet.

Professor Lessing was busy in a corner of the room. She was fussing over racks of equipment. She twiddled knobs and made final adjustments, humming a little tune to herself as she worked.

Hammond wanted to scream and run out of there. Everything felt unreal. He couldn't believe he was doing this.

Project Osiris. Dead bodies being zapped with electricity. High-tech blood running through their veins.

He forced himself to stay put. Major Carr had said, "This job is the sort of thing that could well get your career back on track." Hammond knew he had to keep that in mind.

This was his chance to prove once again how much of a good, loyal soldier he could be.

At last Professor Lessing was ready. She handed a small black box to Hammond. It was the size of a TV remote and had two buttons on it.

"Hand-held control unit," she said. "The green button activates the bodies. The red button shuts them down."

"But how am I supposed to make the bodies move?" Hammond asked. "Shouldn't there be a joy-stick or something?"

Professor Lessing shook her head and smiled. "It isn't a video game, sergeant. These are men. What does one do when one is training men?

"Teach them to follow commands."

"Correct."

Professor Lessing stepped back.

Hammond put his thumb over the green button. He hesitated. This was mad. At the touch of a button, the dead men would get up and walk? No, that couldn't happen.

Then he remembered how one of them had grabbed his wrist. Professor Lessing had told him that this was a reflex action. Sometimes, even when the corpses were supposed to be "switched off", they stirred and moved. It was all to do with tiny amounts of excess electricity in their bodies. It was a bit like a short-circuit, a sudden spark firing through their systems.

The green button would trigger the corpses' battery packs, which would send a jolt of electricity into their brains.

Hammond pressed it, a part of him hoping that it would fail.

It seemed as if his prayer was answered. Nothing happened. Not one of the corpses moved.

Hammond looked round at Professor Lessing.

"Give it a moment," she said.

Then there was a rustle of clothing. A hand twitched. A foot shifted.

One after another, slowly, silently, the dead men rose from the trolleys. They slid their legs over the edge. They got up.

For a while the dead men stood beside the trolleys, swaying a little. Their heads turned on their necks with a creak. Their pale eyes gazed around. It was as if they were taking stock of where they were.

But how can that be? thought Hammond. *They aren't alive. They can't want to know where they are.*

Or can they?

"Look at them," said Professor Lessing. There was wonder in her voice, and pride. "We haven't put battle-dress on them before.

They really look the part, don't they? Proper soldiers." She could have been a mother, talking about how smart and clever her children were.

Hammond could not share her pride. The corpses looked horrible to him. The uniforms hung loosely off their bony frames. The corpses' shoulders were slouched. Their jaws were slack. They were a grim mockery of how soldiers should be.

Then, all at once, the dead men began to walk.

They shuffled forward, their arms swinging by their sides. Their boots scraped the floor. One of the corpses let out a soft moan. Another did the same.

Hammond moved his thumb to the red button on the control unit. The corpses were heading right at him and Professor Lessing. He wanted to stop them.

Professor Lessing said, "No, don't do that. Don't shut them down."

"But they're coming our way." Hammond felt panic. He couldn't help it.

"Use your voice," she urged. "Make them obey you."

"But how ...?"

"The nanobots inside them give them a form of intelligence," said Professor Lessing. "Their brains work at the most basic level. They will respond to certain words, a certain tone of voice. You must take charge of them. Show them who's boss."

Hammond didn't think it would work. But he had nothing to lose by trying.

Holding his thumb ready over the red button, he said, "Halt."

The dead men didn't halt. They continued to shuffle towards him. Their mouths opened and closed. They were all moaning now. It was creepy the way the sound echoed inside the bunker. Hammond could hardly bear to listen to it.

"Once more," said Professor Lessing. "Show them who's boss. Speak like you're speaking to a dog."

"Halt!" said Hammond firmly.

To his surprise, the corpses halted.

They stood in a ragged line. They were no longer moaning. Those pale eyes of theirs were fixed on Hammond. The corpses seemed attracted by him, keen to know what he was going to say next.

Hammond felt a mad laugh bubbling up inside him. He fought it down.

"Walk," he said to the corpses.

There was a pause, then one of them lurched forwards and started to walk. The others followed suit.

"Halt," Hammond said again.

They came to a standstill once more.

"About-turn," he said.

He thought that this might be asking too much of them. But a couple of the corpses did as he asked. They swivelled slowly on the spot. Then the rest did too.

"Quick march."

The dead men shuffled all the way to the far end of the bunker. Hammond waited to see if they would bump into the wall, but they stopped just short of it. They stood facing the wall, as if waiting for the next order from Hammond.

"You see?" said Professor Lessing. "They do just as they're told, yet they still have a few simple instincts. They'll do what you want but they're not stupid. They're the perfect soldiers. And that's not all. Bring them back here and I'll show you something."

Hammond ordered the dead men to about-turn and walk back. As they did so, Professor Lessing searched in the pocket of her lab coat. She pulled out a small pistol, a Walther P99.

Hammond looked shocked. "What on earth are you doing with that?"

"Don't worry," said Professor Lessing. "I don't carry it around with me all the time. Just for special events. Cover your ears."

She cocked the pistol, took aim and fired.

The bullet hit one of the corpses smack in the chest. The dead man reeled, but then went on walking.

She fired the Walther three more times. Hammond had his fingers in his ears, but even so, his head rang from the gunshots.

Three more bullet holes appeared in the dead man's shirt. No blood came out, just little dribbles of black oozy liquid. The dead man looked down at his front, as if puzzled. But he still kept going. He stopped only when Hammond told all of the corpses to stop.

"No harm done," said Professor Lessing, pointing to the corpse she had shot. "I was using small-calibre bullets, I admit. But we've tried out rifle rounds as well. They pass right through, and if you take care not to hit a leg joint, the corpses can still walk."

Her eyes gleamed behind her glasses.

"They feel no pain," she said. "They don't need feeding or paying. As long as their batteries are charged up, they plod on. They're the fighting force of the future, Sergeant Hammond! The next wave of troops. And they're ours!"

Hammond glanced at the row of dead men. He could see Professor Lessing's point.

He wasn't sure, however, if everything was really as amazing as the professor seemed to think.

Chapter 7

Software Programmer

Hammond spent weeks in the bunker with the dead men. He worked hard, getting them to follow commands that were more and more complex. He taught them to raise their arms. He taught them right and left. He got them to march in time, walking in two rows of five. After a couple of months he even had the dead men giving a salute.

Each morning he went into the bunker with a shudder. Hammond couldn't forget that he was working every day with dead bodies. It was bizarre. It was revolting. He must be crazy to keep doing this.

But then the job took over. Hammond focused on training the corpses, and his queasy feelings went away.

It was strange how something so far beyond ordinary everyday life could, after a while, become normal.

The days became shorter. Winter set in. Hammond hardly noticed. He'd lost track of time passing. He arrived at Wild Hare Park in darkness each morning and left again in darkness each evening. He had a room at a Holiday Inn a few miles away, but the world outside the Vault didn't seem important any more. It was just a place to sleep. The Vault was where it all happened. Hammond didn't even notice when Christmas came and went. The same with New Year. His life was underground, in the neon-lit Vault, with the corpses.

After a while Hammond found he'd stopped thinking of the corpses as dead things. He'd started to see them as individuals.

Each corpse had his own habits. Each was a different character.

For instance, one of them was smarter than the rest. He learned Hammond's commands faster than the others. He picked up on what to do, and the other nine dead men then copied him.

Hammond gave this one a nickname. He called the corpse "Chief".

Another of the corpses walked with a slight limp. Hammond decided to call him "Gimpy".

One of the dead men was missing a finger. He became known as "Niner".

Then there was "Lofty", the shortest of the ten corpses. "Slowcoach". "Charlie Chomp", who always clacked his teeth together. "Earring". "Mr Wallace", because he reminded Hammond of one his old schoolmasters, Mr Wallace, who had taught him geography in Year Eleven. "Ozzy Osbourne" was the one who made the most noise, moaning almost all the time. And the last one was called "Baz", because Hammond hadn't ever known a squad of soldiers without at least one Baz among them.

Professor Lessing was amused that Hammond had chosen names for the corpses.

"They're like pets, aren't they?" she said. "You get quite fond of them."

Hammond didn't agree. He didn't think he was fond of the dead men. But the names made it easier to deal with them on a daily basis.

What also made it easier was knowing about the nanobots inside the dead men. Hammond could tell himself that it wasn't the actual corpses who were learning how to be soldiers. It was the "liquid computers" inside them that were learning. So he wasn't a drill instructor for the living dead; he was in fact a kind of software programmer.

One morning in January, Hammond woke up in his hotel room and noticed something.

He'd stopped having dreams about Kurdistan.

He looked back over the past few weeks and found he had slept well every night. He hadn't woken up in a sweat, with screams and gunfire echoing through his head.

He hated to admit it, but maybe Major Carr had been right. This job was just what he needed. He was putting Kurdistan behind him. He was moving on.

For the first time in six years, Hammond felt almost happy.

Chapter 8

Live-firing Exercise

In the canteen one lunchtime, Professor Lessing had some news for Hammond.

"Everyone's really impressed with what you've been doing, Dex," she said. "So much so that they want you to put on a demo. They want you to put your lads through their paces, in front of several very important people. How about that?"

"I don't know, Ruth," said Hammond. He and the professor were on first-name terms now. They had developed a respect for each other, although Hammond still found Professor Lessing a little hard to like. She was such a private person. She kept herself to herself.

"I'm not sure we're ready for something like that," he went on. "Slowcoach still isn't as fast as the others, and Gimpy doesn't really understand 'stand at ease'. And as for Mr Wallace's gun-handling skills ..."

"Nonsense!" snorted Professor Lessing. "You've got those ten quite under control."

"They make mistakes."

"You're too close to them, that's what's wrong. What you see as mistakes are really nothing more than minor glitches. You can do this demo, Dex. I know you can."

Professor Lessing's faith in Hammond gave Hammond faith in himself.

"Yeah," he said. "All right. Maybe I can."

His face clouded.

"There is one thing that's been bugging me, though," he said.

"What's that?" she said.

"I shouldn't ask, but after all this time I think I have a right to know."

"Go on."

"Where did they come from?" he asked.

"What do you mean?" said Professor Lessing. She had a very slight frown on her face.

"My ten corpses," said Hammond. "Who were they when they were alive?"

Professor Lessing shunted some peas around her plate with a fork.

"Well," she said at last, "you know how some people sign forms saying they want to leave their bodies to medical science after

they die? They offer them for research.
That's what your lot did."

"Did they have any idea this was how they
would end up?" Hammond asked. "As
soldiers?"

"Really, Dex," said Professor Lessing
sharply. "You shouldn't think about it. Let's
drop the subject. You should focus your mind
on getting your men in shape for the demo."

She finished her lunch in a hurry and left
the canteen.

A few days later, Hammond led his dead
men outside. The audience of VIPs was
waiting. It was made up of generals and high-
ranking Ministry of Defence officials,
including the Secretary of State himself.
They stood on a hilltop at a safe distance,
watching through binoculars.

It was a live-firing exercise, meaning that
there were real bullets loaded in the corpses'

rifles. Before now, the corpses had fired only blanks, in the bunker.

Of course, Hammond was nervous. He couldn't afford for anything to go wrong. The fate of the whole project was riding on this demo. The army had invested a lot of money in Project Osiris. If things didn't go smoothly today, then the top brass might close it down.

But the corpses performed well. First of all, Hammond marched them up and down on the grass. Then he ordered them to kneel and fire at targets. Almost every shot found its mark. Lastly Hammond got the dead men in an attack formation. They jogged forwards, two by two. The ones at the rear covered the ones in front with their rifles. Hammond chucked thunder-flashes and flares at them as they came. The corpses didn't flinch.

When it was all over, the sound of clapping drifted down from the crowd of bigwigs on the hilltop. Hammond lined up the dead men and made them salute.

He looked at the corpses as they stood there with their hands beside their heads. He noticed that Chief had turned his eyes upwards and seemed to be looking at the sky. It was a beautiful spring day, and this was the first time, as far as Hammond knew, that his corpses had been outdoors. The sun shone on their withered faces. Was that a smile on Earring's lips? Goddammit, was that a tear shining in the corner of Charlie Chomp's eye?

Hammond told himself that this was madness.

They were dead.

Sunshine and blue skies meant nothing to them.

How stupid can you be!

Chapter 9

Not the Zombie Squad

Hammond shut the corpses down, and men in the white plastic suits began to wheel them back underground. Then Hammond saw someone walk down towards him from the hilltop. It was Major Carr.

"Bravo!" said Carr. "That was a huge success. You did it. The chaps up there are very excited, sergeant. You should hear what they're saying. Myself, I had my doubts. I'll admit that now. I wasn't 100 per cent sure you were up to the job. But you've proved me wrong."

Hammond gave a slight nod. "Thank you, sir."

Carr looked stouter than ever. His cheeks bulged like red apples. Not only had he got much fatter, but there seemed to be even more medals on his chest, as well.

Carr glanced at one of the dead men, Niner, who was being trundled past on a trolley. "Brrr. I don't envy you, working with stiffs all day long. But still, you've done great work. Let me tell you, my friend: you and your Zombie Squad are going places."

"I'm sorry?" Hammond said. "Me and my – what?"

"We've been trying to come up with a name for them," Carr said. "Your dead chaps. Zombie Squad seemed to fit the bill. Why? What's the problem? Don't you like it?"

"Not really. It seems a bit ... harsh to me."

"Oh." Carr blinked. "Interesting. You think it might hurt their feelings, being called zombies?" He grinned, but it looked more like a sneer than a grin.

"No, I don't think it's the right name, that's all," said Hammond. "Zombies have no mind of their own. My lot have, as I've just proved."

"So what would you call them, if you had to give them a name?"

Hammond considered for a moment. This wasn't something he'd thought about before.

"The Dead Brigade," he said.

Carr was confused. "I'll grant you the 'dead' part, but brigade?" he said. "A brigade is several regiments, not ten men. I thought you wanted to get it right."

"It sounds OK," Hammond said. "And who knows, maybe in the future there will be a whole brigade of them."

"Good point," said Carr. "Well, this is your baby. The Dead Brigade it is. I'll let everyone know that that's their new name. No more mention of zombies." He made a zipping-lips gesture. "*Zombie* will be a bad word from now on."

There was a twinkle in his eyes. Hammond knew Carr was laughing at him. When Carr went back to rejoin the VIPs on the hill, he would make jokes about the name. That was what senior officers did amongst themselves. They liked to poke fun at the junior ranks – although only when the junior ranks weren't around to hear.

Hammond didn't care. It worked the other way round too.

"Anyway," said Carr, "today has been a great success. Don't be surprised if you get a

call some time in the next few days, sergeant.
Your Zom – " He stopped himself. "Your
Dead Brigade is likely to be sent into action
soon. I mean it. The generals are keen to get
your chaps out in the field, while they're still
fresh." Carr chuckled. "As fresh, that is, as
dead things can be."

Chapter 10

Montana

The Chinook helicopter roared above the rolling green hills of Montana, USA. Inside, Hammond sat with his Dead Brigade. He was dressed in layers of thick clothing but he was still shivering. The cabin of the helicopter had been adapted to transport these soldiers of his. It had been lined with insulation, and a carbon dioxide cooling unit had been installed. The cabin was now, in fact, like one huge fridge. The ten corpses lay there on cots, with their battery packs hooked up to a central charging unit. Hammond could have travelled up front in the cockpit, where there was heating. But he preferred to be with his men, so that he could keep an eye on them during the flight.

The Chinook's pilot landed the chopper 10 kilometres from the target zone. Hammond stripped off his outer layers. Then, wearing his camouflage C95 combats, he led the dead men down the tail ramp. They made for their goal at a fast pace, trekking through pine forests and across shallow rivers. The sun was setting. Flies swarmed around the corpses, and around Hammond too. Only Hammond was bothered by them. The dead men didn't notice, even though it was their smell that was driving the flies wild.

When night fell, the enemy was in sight.

The mission was a search-and-retrieve job. A group of far-right lunatics had got hold of some VX nerve gas. They had bought a canister of the gas from an arms dealer working for a rogue state in the Middle East. There was enough of the VX to kill thousands of people, if it was released in the middle of a city.

The far-right lunatics, who called themselves the White Sons of Purity, were holding the US government to ransom. They said they would let off the gas unless every single black person in America was shipped off to Africa.

Of course the president refused to go along with this crazy demand. "I do not give in to terrorists," she said. "Most of all not in an election year."

The Pentagon, however, was worried about sending any of its soldiers in to attack the White Sons of Purity. It was too risky. The nerve gas might be released during the fighting. If the wind was blowing the wrong way, a number of small towns round about would be wiped out. US army special forces were on stand-by, ready to go in. But they would be used only as a last resort. For the moment, the president was hoping to reach some kind of agreement with the White Sons.

It was a tense stand-off that had lasted for several days. Then the British government stepped in with an offer of help. The British army, after all, had ten soldiers who could not be harmed by the deadly gas.

The Americans did not believe this but they said yes anyway. Sure. Why not? Give it a shot. Send some Brits in. If they pulled it off, great. If not, then better that British soldiers should be killed than American soldiers. And if things went really wrong, the president would have someone else to blame. She would win whatever happened.

Now Hammond waited till the moon was high. It shone down on the compound where the White Sons were holed up. The compound covered a wide area of hillside and was surrounded by a chain-link fence five metres high. There were a dozen tin-roofed shacks and barns within the compound. The gas canister was hidden in one of the barns. At present, two White Sons were on guard duty outside the barn door. They were carrying sub-machine guns and wore grenade belts around their chests. They were beefy-looking men with long beards.

The Dead Brigade had ear-pieces in their ears. Hammond had a mike strapped to his throat. This gave him a comms link with his men. He could whisper orders in their ears.

Hammond put on a respirator, just in case. Then he gave the order to move in.

US special forces had done a recon of the area. They'd found that there was an alarm system hidden all round the outside of the White Sons' compound. The alarm system used thermal sensors to warn if anyone was getting close. The heat signal of a human body would trigger them, and bells would ring inside the compound.

Hammond had been warned about the alarm system.

But he wasn't worried.

His soldiers, after all, didn't give off any heat.

Chief reached the fence. Neither of the White Sons guards spotted him. Chief cut a hole in the fence with wire clippers.

Then Baz and Earring ducked through the hole. They crossed the compound towards the barn, keeping to the shadows. Hammond, watching from a small hill some way off, guided them via the comms link.

The two White Sons guards caught sight of Baz and Earring at the last moment. Through long-range night vision goggles, Hammond saw the guards' faces. There was confusion first. But soon confusion turned to horror, as the guards saw that it wasn't a pair of soldiers they were looking at – it was a pair of walking corpses.

The guards overcame their horror, but too late. Before they could cock their guns, Baz and Earring attacked them. They slit the White Sons' throats with knives. The dead killed the living.

Gimpy and Charlie Chomp then went into the barn and got the gas canister out. The other eight covered for them while they were doing this.

Carrying their prize, the Dead Brigade left the compound through the hole in the fence. It looked as if they were going to make a clean get-away.

Then: a stroke of bad luck.

A White Son came out of one of the shacks. He was planning to take a piss outdoors. He went towards the fence, unzipping his trousers ... and saw the Dead Brigade on the other side of the wire, making off with the VX gas.

Hammond held his breath. He was sure the White Son was going to raise the alarm. Over the comms link he told the Brigade to make for the trees, pronto.

The dead men did as they were told. All except Chief.

Hammond watched Chief turn and raise his pistol. The gun had a silencer fitted to the barrel. In a calm and casual manner, Chief aimed. The gun went pfft! The bullet hit the White Son slap bang in the fore-head. The man keeled over. He hit the ground, dead, without uttering a word.

Hammond nearly cheered.

On the way back to the helicopter, however, a sickening thought came to his mind.

Chief had done the right thing, and saved the mission.

But Hammond hadn't ordered Chief to shoot the man.

Chapter 11

Nairobi

The dictator stepped out onto the balcony of his mansion. He was wearing red slippers and a pair of satin pyjamas with a zebra-stripe pattern. The hot night air simmered around him. His bald, brown head was shiny with sweat.

Nairobi lay spread out before him, dark. The street lights were out. House lights weren't working either, except in a few places like the dictator's mansion, which had its own power supply.

Kenya's capital city had gone to rack and ruin in recent months, ever since the dictator had seized power. He'd murdered the president with his bare hands, and had his men kill several members of the National Assembly. Now Nairobi, along with the rest of Kenya, was a lawless place. Nothing worked properly any more. People were starving. They were fighting over scraps of food. There was a rumour that some of them had even begun to eat their own babies, they were so hungry and desperate.

But all was quiet in the city right now, so quiet that even the crickets weren't chirping. The silence was, to the dictator, the silence of fear. He listened to it, and it made him feel secure. Here he was, in his vast mansion, which had once belonged to a manager from a Chinese oil company. He was surrounded by armed soldiers. The people of Kenya feared him, and sometimes fear could turn to hate. But even if the people rose up against him, they couldn't get at him.

The dictator's thoughts turned to what was going on up in the north-east of the country, beyond the Great Rift Valley. There, Kenyans were fleeing in their hundreds across the border into Uganda. The Ugandan government was not happy about this. They didn't want all these refugees coming into their country. Uganda was making threats of war against Kenya.

Go ahead, the dictator said to himself with a grin.

A war with Uganda would be good for him. It would make his rule stronger. It would frighten the people of his country, and that meant he could tighten his grip on Kenya even harder.

There was a sudden rattle of gunfire, close by. The dictator jumped. The sound came from the courtyard right below where he was standing. He heard someone cry out. It was one of his body-guards. The man was yelling something about the dead. The dead were walking ...!

The body-guard let out an awful choking cry. Then he fell silent.

More gunfire followed. The dictator saw muzzle flashes in the dark. There were yells and howls. A small but fierce battle was going on in the grounds of his mansion.

The dictator decided he would be much safer indoors. He went back into his bedroom, calling out the names of the two soldiers who were on guard duty outside the door.

There was no reply. The door was wide open. In the corridor, the dictator could just see the legs of someone lying on the floor.

And in the room itself were three men who shouldn't have been there – three soldiers. One of them stood on the lion-skin rug that lay near the bed, his boots rucking up the animal's golden skin.

The dictator knew those uniforms. They were British.

Then he looked at their faces.

His jaw dropped. His whole body shook with fear.

It couldn't be!

The three soldiers shuffled towards him, moaning softly. The dictator was too terrified to move. He felt something warm and wet at his crotch. Urine trickled down his legs, soaking through his pyjamas.

Two of the soldiers grabbed him. Their fingers were hard and cold. The third soldier levelled a pistol at the dictator's head. The dictator begged God to have mercy on him. He prayed for this not to happen.

Hammond, who was looking on from a rooftop 500 metres away, gave the order.

The dictator screamed, and his scream was cut off by a single gunshot.

A truck had been parked in an alley behind the mansion. It was waiting. All ten of the Dead Brigade made their way to it, as soon as the job was done.

Hammond joined them. He drove the truck through the city and out into the country. Dawn broke suddenly over the African landscape, the sunlight revealing grassy plains dotted with low trees. The truck reached the meeting point with the helicopter. The Chinook took off, and Hammond settled the dead men in their cots and switched them off with the portable control unit.

The flight back to RAF Brize Norton was long and bumpy. Hammond tried not to think about the dictator's final scream. It had been an execution, and the man had deserved it. The dictator was a monster, famous for torturing his enemies to death. He was lucky that his own death had been so quick and clean.

He was gone now, at any rate. And so there would be no war between Kenya and Uganda.

A job well done.

The Chinook made a stop-over in Gibraltar to fill up with fuel.

Shortly after that, in the air above Spain, Ozzy Osbourne started to moan.

Hammond checked the hand-held control. He pressed the red button twice.

The Dead Brigade were shut down, he was sure. All of them. They shouldn't be active in any way.

But still, Ozzy Osbourne moaned. His voice was half drowned by the thunder of the Chinook's rotors.

He was crying out.

He was speaking words.

Hammond felt his skin crawl. Ozzy was talking. Hammond couldn't be quite sure of this, since there was so much other noise in the helicopter cabin. Even so, he was pretty certain.

Ozzy was saying, "No. No. No."

The same word, over and over.

"No. No. No."

Chapter 12

Belgrade

The terrorists had taken over a hospital in Dedinje, a posh suburb of Belgrade. They were holding doctors, nurses and patients as hostages. They had wired up the building with bombs.

The terrorists' leader was on trial for war crimes. He had recently been captured, after many years on the run. During the Balkan war in the 1990s, the leader had done a number of vile acts. The worst thing he'd done was to burn down a school with all the children inside. The children had belonged to a different ethnic group from the one the leader belonged to. That was all they had done wrong.

The terrorists wanted their leader to be set free. They demanded that the trial should be halted and that he should be released without charge. Otherwise they would blow up the hospital and everyone in it, including themselves.

Serbian police had surrounded the hospital. For two days they had tried to talk to the terrorists via a hot-line. Sometimes the terrorists responded, but when they did, it was only to give the police their list of demands again.

Time was running out. The terrorists had set a dead-line. Six hours were left. If their leader wasn't a free man by then – *BOOM*.

A large, black refrigerator van appeared. It drove slowly towards the hospital. The police had set up a cordon around the hospital and put up road blocks everywhere. The van braked at the road block and the driver spoke to the police. The police then got on the phone to the terrorists. They managed to talk the terrorists into letting the van go all the way up to the hospital.

After all, it was just a refrigerator van from a funeral home. Inside it were some bodies that had to be dropped off at the morgue in the hospital's basement. The funeral home didn't have the space for them. The bodies would rot if they weren't put in the morgue fast.

The terrorists checked the van when it arrived. They suspected this was some sort of trick. The van driver and his assistant showed them ten dead bodies stacked in the back of the vehicle. The terrorists studied the bodies with care. One of them got out a knife. He jabbed it into each of the bodies in turn, just to make sure. Yes. They were quite dead.

The van driver and his assistant were allowed to take the bodies down to the morgue. They left them in a cold-storage room.

As the van drew away from the hospital, the driver's assistant breathed a sigh of relief.

"Phew," said Hammond. "We made it."

The van driver sitting next to Hammond was in fact from MI6. He had been based in the Balkan region for years. He spoke several of the local languages like a native.

He said to Hammond, "You know, I've heard rumours about Project Osiris, but I'd never have believed a word of it till today. Do you honestly think those ten corpses can resolve this crisis?"

Hammond gave a knowing smile. "Just you wait and see."

The count-down to the terrorists' dead-line ticked by.

With less than an hour to go before the bombs went off, the police began hearing shouts of alarm from inside the hospital.

A short while later, two of the terrorists came running out of the main entrance. The two men looked scared out of their wits. The police gunned them down on the spot.

Outside the police cordon, Hammond waited. As far as he could tell, everything was going according to plan. The Dead Brigade were up and about. They'd broken out of the cold-storage room and were hunting down the terrorists.

But Hammond had no way of seeing what the dead men were doing, and he wasn't in touch with them via a comms link. The Dead Brigade didn't have their ear-pieces on. It had needed to look as if the corpses in the black van were the real thing. Therefore they couldn't have ear-pieces, or guns, or anything except the white hospital gowns they were wearing.

Hammond had, to a certain extent, been putting on a show for the MI6 man earlier. He was not as confident as he pretended to be. He became more concerned with every passing moment. The Dead Brigade were on their own.

Hammond had spent 24 hours coaching them for this mission, running them through take-down plans in the bunker at the Vault. He had directed them endless times through a full-size mock-up of the hospital floor plan. He was sure they knew what to do. But he wished, for their sake, that they could have had him to guide them.

What if something went wrong?

Something did.

Several of the hospital windows blew out at the same time. Broken glass rained into the street below. The sound of the blast reached Hammond seconds later.

Flames flickered from the shattered windows. Smoke poured out.

The police knew they had no choice but to storm the hospital.

They went in, guns at the ready.

What they found inside was all of the terrorists dead and all of the hostages alive. Only one of the bombs had gone off. The fire brigade was waiting on stand-by and the fire was soon under control.

All but one of the terrorists had either been strangled or had their necks broken. The hostages couldn't give a clear picture of what had gone on just before the police went in. It had been chaos and confusion for a while. Several of the hostages claimed to have seen white-robed men in the corridors, killing the terrorists with their bare hands. The last terrorist left alive had panicked and set off the bomb. He had died in the explosion.

The stories about white-robed men seemed too wild to be true. The police decided that the hostages had made them up. What really must have happened was that the terrorists had got spooked. They had started killing one another by mistake.

Later, Hammond and the MI6 man returned to the hospital in the black van. Again they pretended to be from the funeral home, and the police let them in.

To Hammond's dismay, only eight of the Dead Brigade were in the cold-storage room. Two of them, Gimpy and Mr Wallace, hadn't made it back there. Hammond could only think they had been blown up by the bomb.

Of the remaining eight, three were damaged. Slowcoach had lost an arm from the elbow down. Lofty and Earring had burn marks all over them. These three must also have been caught in the explosion.

It was a glum Hammond who flew home with his troops. The mission was a success. But the Dead Brigade had taken its first casualties.

Chapter 13

The Sleep of the Dead

Dreams of Kurdistan returned. Everyone at Wild Hare Park kept praising Hammond for the Belgrade job. He felt a failure. For three nights in a row, the dreams were as vivid as they had ever been. Hammond knew why. He had lost men again, and he felt it was his fault. The events in the Balkans had stirred up his memories of the events in Kurdistan. He'd thought all that was behind him. He'd thought the killings in the Zagros mountains were safely dead and buried.

But the past, it seemed, could never die. Even when it looked dead, all it was doing was lying quiet, as if waiting for someone to press a button and bring it back to life.

Hammond found something to do whenever the dream woke him up. He headed over to Wild Hare Park and went down into the Vault. There, in the Project Osiris room, he watched the Dead Brigade lying on their beds, recharging their batteries. They were so still and quiet. He drew comfort from how they looked. They looked at peace.

Hammond's mother used to have a saying. If someone was really fast asleep, she would say they were sleeping the sleep of the dead.

The Dead Brigade were doing just that.

Hammond kept a close eye on Ozzy Osbourne. There had been no repeat of the episode in the helicopter on the way back from Africa. Ozzy hadn't cried out again when he was supposed to be shut down. At least, as far as Hammond knew it hadn't happened again.

Hammond had thought about saying something to Professor Lessing. He'd also thought about telling her how Chief had shot the White Son without being told to.

But he had decided to keep quiet about both these things. He didn't want to cause trouble. He remembered what Major Carr had said about "rocking the boat". Hammond was proud of his work with the Dead Brigade. He and his troops were gaining a good name within the army. He'd been given a second chance and he didn't want to blow it.

One night, at three o'clock in the morning, Hammond entered the Project Osiris room, and found Professor Lessing there. She was hard at work. Hammond soon saw what she was doing.

Two new bodies had arrived. Professor Lessing was hooking up their batteries.

Hammond then noticed something else.

Slowcoach had a new arm, to replace the one he'd lost in the Balkans.

There was a ragged purple scar line around Slowcoach's elbow. Steel staples held the new part of the arm in place.

Hammond looked closer. The new arm had a marking on it. Just above the wrist there was a small blue tattoo.

The tattoo was a parachute with feathered wings on either side of it.

Hammond knew that symbol, and let out a small gasp.

Professor Lessing was so busy with her work, she hadn't heard Hammond enter the room. Now she turned round.

"Ah, Dex," she said. Her eyes flicked to one side. She looked sly, like a child caught stealing.

"This was going to be a surprise for you in the morning," Professor Lessing said. "Two new troops for you to train."

"Well, it's a surprise for me now," Hammond said. "I see you've fixed Slowcoach."

"I hope the transplant will work," Professor Lessing said, pointing to Slowcoach's arm. "There's no reason why it shouldn't. With a living person, there's the immune system to worry about. Living bodies sometimes reject new organs. But with the dead that isn't a factor. We'll know in a day or two whether the transplant 'takes' or not. I think it will, and Slowcoach will be good as new. It's the next step in our plans for the perfect soldier. We can repair them as they go. Not bad, eh?"

She looked at him.

"What's the problem, Dex?"

Hammond said, "I'll tell you what the problem is. That tattoo."

Professor Lessing glanced at the tattoo, then looked back at Hammond.

"It's the symbol of the Parachute Regiment," Hammond said. "That arm came from a soldier."

Professor Lessing stood still for a few seconds. Then she sighed.

"So maybe there's something you're not telling me here, Ruth," Hammond said. "Maybe you haven't been quite honest with me."

"You're right," said Professor Lessing. "You were bound to find out sooner or later. It might as well be now. Just be prepared. I'm going to tell you the truth, the whole truth, and it isn't pleasant."

Chapter 14

Recycling

In her stuffy, messy little study, Professor Lessing poured out brandy.

"Alcohol at three in the morning," she said. "Shocking."

She gave one glass of brandy to Hammond. She drank the other herself.

Hammond waited for her to start talking. Professor Lessing seemed not to know where to begin. At last she spoke.

"Put simply," she said, "your Dead Brigade are ex-soldiers."

"Ex?" said Hammond. "As in discharged? Retired?"

"As in dead. Killed in action."

"Killed."

"They are the ones who come home in body bags," Professor Lessing said. "The ones who leave behind weeping wives and children without dads. The ones whose cars go over landmines buried in the road. The ones who take a sniper bullet through the heart and never even hear the gunshot. The ones who just have some stupid accident while out on exercises – trip and fall and break their necks. The ones whose parachutes don't open fully during a jump. The unlucky ones."

Hammond had a hard time believing what he was hearing. "And they get buried with full honours, and then later someone comes along and digs them up for you?"

"No," said Professor Lessing. "They don't even get buried. In each case, a coffin is lowered into the ground, but what's in the coffin isn't a body. It's sandbags, or rocks, something like that, I'm not sure of the exact details. It's not part of my job. There's something in the coffin, at any rate, that weighs as much as a body. The body itself, meanwhile, is transported to Wild Hare Park, and we keep it on ice in the Vault until we can start work on it."

"So the dead man's family don't know their loved one isn't in the coffin," said Hammond.

"Of course not. It's a cruel trick, I know that. But it has to be done."

"But couldn't you tell the family what the body's going to be used for? Ask their permission, even?"

"They'd never give it, would they?" said Professor Lessing. "And besides, Project

Osiris is top secret. We can't have the public finding out what we're getting up to here. It's better that we just take the bodies rather than ask for them. That way there's far less risk of the truth getting out."

"What people don't know won't hurt them, eh?" said Hammond.

"That's how we have to play it, Dex," said Professor Lessing. "Trust me, if there was another way of doing this, I'd have gone for it. But there isn't another way. At least, not one that I can work out."

"How about those people who sign forms and leave their bodies to medical science? You know, the ones you lied to me about."

"Not a good source. Too much paperwork involved. If we keep it within the army, we keep things simple."

"All the same ..."

"Listen, Dex," Professor Lessing said firmly. "Without those bodies there'd be no

Project Osiris, and no Dead Brigade. Simple as that. We need them. We need cleanly killed corpses, ones that've had as little damage done to them as possible. We need them to make sure the British army survives and the world remains a safe place."

"Yeah?" said Hammond in bitter tones.

"Yes," said the professor, "and you know it. You can huff and puff about it all you like. You can act all indignant. But deep down, you can't really think of a decent argument against it, can you? A dead soldier's body is a dead soldier's body. It's no use to anyone ... except us. We have a source of them, right on our very door-step, as it were. It makes perfect sense to use it."

She gave a brittle laugh.

"You could call it recycling, if you like," she said. "That's all the rage these days, isn't it? The army has gone green."

Hammond did not even pretend to smile.

"Those are people," he said. "Human beings. They didn't say they were willing to have this done to them."

"They *were* people, Dex," Professor Lessing said, putting him right. "Past tense. Now, they're just empty shells. They're needed to house the nanobots. That's all."

Hammond paused, then said, "No. They *are* people."

"What do you mean?"

He took a deep breath, then said, "I think they're still alive, Ruth. I don't know how, but I think there's still something in those bodies, some spark of the men they used to be."

"What makes you say that?" Professor Lessing asked.

"Well ..."

Hammond told her about Chief acting of his own accord, shooting without being ordered to; and then about Ozzy crying out, "No. No. No," in the helicopter. He also described how some of the Dead Brigade had turned their faces up to the sun, that day they went outdoors for the first time.

Hammond wanted to shock Professor Lessing. In a way, he was seeking revenge. She'd warned him that the truth wouldn't be nice, and it wasn't. He was angry with her for sharing this with him, even though he'd asked to be told. He would have been happier never knowing that the army was re-using its dead.

"So they're not just empty shells, though you might think so," he ended up saying. "Horrible as it sounds, the Dead Brigade are somehow aware of what they are – what you've made them."

Hammond expected that Professor Lessing would be upset. He was even hoping she might start to cry.

But all she did was fix him with an even stare, and say, "I know."

Chapter 15

A Good Reason for Brandy

"I've heard Ozzy call out, just as you describe," Professor Lessing said. "Remember, Dex, I spend as much time with the Dead Brigade as you do. Maybe more. When you're not with them, training or out on a mission, who's looking after them? Me."

She gulped down her glass of brandy and poured herself some more.

"Ozzy's not the only one, either," she continued. "Charlie Chomp groans from time to time. Just one word, and it really sounds like a woman's name. Sarah. He says that, and it's like he's hoping she'll hear him. He's hoping Sarah, whoever she is, will come and help him. It gave me chills the first time I heard it, let me tell you." More of the brandy went down her throat. Hammond had wondered why Professor Lessing kept a bottle of the stuff in her study. Now he knew why.

"I've thought about it long and hard," she said. "Why are they doing it? They're dead. Some of them have been dead for months. The only things putting life into those corpses are electricity and the nanobot blood. How can they speak? How come they know words? How did Chief know he had to shoot that man?"

"Instinct?" Hammond suggested. "If they were soldiers before they died, they might still have some of that training instinct in their bodies." He shook his head. "No, that's crazy."

"Not all crazy," said Professor Lessing. "There is such a thing as muscle memory. People develop it when they use their bodies for one activity a lot. Athletes, for example, and dancers. They train hard and often, and their muscles learn to 'remember' what they're meant to do. After a while, the muscles perform almost without the brain telling them to. The athlete hardly needs to think about running or jumping. His body does it anyway. The dancer goes through her steps without having to remind herself of every move, every twirl, every arm lift. The mind stops controlling the body. The body takes over."

"Sort of like an auto-pilot."

"Sort of." Professor Lessing rubbed her chin. "But, in the case of the Dead Brigade, muscle memory doesn't explain how they can talk. Speech is a brain function."

"Maybe we only think they're talking," Hammond said. "Maybe a random sound is coming from their throats and we think it's a word we recognise."

"Of course. Humans have a habit of finding patterns. We look for them, even when they're not there. We like to make sense of the world, and patterns help us do that. But – our dead men are going to a lot of effort to speak. They're sucking air into their lungs, air they don't need to breathe. Then they're pushing it out again, and making their mouths shape words at the same time. That can't be just chance. It's got to be on purpose."

"So where does that leave us?" said Hammond.

"Your guess is as good as mine," said Professor Lessing.

"Well then, I have a possible answer. It's not a very scientific one, though."

Professor Lessing cocked her head. "Let's hear it. Science isn't getting us any nearer the truth. Let's hear what a non-scientist thinks."

Hammond hesitated. "What if it's their souls?" he said. "Their souls are coming back to their bodies. Forget about nanobots and batteries for a moment. What if you really have brought the dead back to life, Ruth?"

There was silence in the study. A long silence.

"If that's so," Professor Lessing said at last, "I don't even want to think about it. It's just too fucking scary for words. And too fucking horrible."

And she poured them both another drink.

Chapter 16

Souls Held Captive

Nineteen days passed without another mission.

Hammond trained the two new corpses. He got them used to weapons and marching. He gave them names: Chalky and Grinner. He made them part of the team. Soon, the Dead Brigade was a unit again, ten soldiers working as one.

Hammond found it hard to look any of his troops in the eye, however. In each of their faces he saw a man who had once been a son, a brother, maybe a husband and a father too. A soldier. A man who, like him, had joined the army, but could never have guessed that this was what the army would do to him after he died, that this was how he would be treated. He wouldn't be allowed to rest in a grave. He would be injected with life again. He would become a puppet, twitching on the end of electric strings.

The thought made Hammond sick.

Inside those corpses lay the buried remains of the men they used to be. Behind those pale, dull eyes, minds were peering out, as if through murky windows.

The Dead Brigade knew what had been done to them. They knew what was happening to their bodies. How they were being used. Abused.

Hammond pictured men in prison. Men behind bars. Souls held captive. All alone. Screaming.

Three weeks later Major Carr came to visit.

Carr arrived at Wild Hare Park full of pomp and energy. He came down into the Vault to see Hammond. He shook Hammond's hand hard, as if pumping up a bicycle tyre.

"Well done, sergeant," he said.

"For what?" asked Hammond.

"I've taken it upon myself to deliver the good news in person," Carr said. "Promotion, my friend. You've won a promotion. A reward for all the brilliant work you've been doing."

"Prom – ?" Hammond hesitated over the word.

"To warrant officer grade two," said Carr. "Quite a leap. Not even stopping off at colour sergeant on the way. Warrant Officer Dex Hammond. Has a nice ring to it, don't you think?"

Warrant Officer Dex Hammond.

Before he came to Wild Hare Park, Hammond would have thought this a dream come true. He'd climbed another rung up the army ladder. He was rising again. It was all he had ever wanted.

Now, though, he wasn't so sure it was what he wanted.

"Of course there'll be an official do," Carr went on. "You'll get given the crown for your sleeve and all that sort of thing. But I just had to tell you now. I couldn't wait. Soon as I heard about it, I came right over. So, what do you say? How do you feel, WO2 Hammond?"

Hammond looked at Carr's fat, flushed face. He stared into his piggy little eyes. This was the man whose rash decision had cost seven soldiers their lives in Kurdistan.

This was Major Carr, who had chosen Hammond for the Project Osiris job, plucking him out of nowhere, almost on a whim. Carr had given Hammond a fresh chance to succeed in the army, yes. He'd helped him. But helped him in a way that put Hammond in his debt. Helped him like a millionaire tossing coins to a beggar.

And now here was Carr bringing news of Hammond's promotion, acting as though this was a gift that was his to give.

Hammond thought of all this, and thought of his Dead Brigade, those tragic creatures who were half aware of their undead state. Dead soldiers trapped in hell.

And he lost it.

He lost his temper.

There was no one else around. Hammond and Carr were alone in one of the Vault's underground corridors. There was no one else to hear and see what happened next.

But Hammond wouldn't have cared even if there had been someone around. He'd have done it anyway.

He shouted at Carr. Roared at him. Rage gushed out. The anger and frustration, which Hammond had bottled up for years, exploded. All his true feelings about Carr poured from him in a torrent of words. He told Carr he was an arse-licking idiot. He told him he was the kind of officer that most soldiers would happily see hanging by his neck from a lamp-post.

He told him all this and more, and he ended by saying, "And you can stick your promotion up your saggy, chair-polishing backside! Sir!"

During this long, loud rant, Major Carr's face got redder and redder. He drew his lips tightly together. His eyes shrank to dots. Carr seemed to swell up. He looked indignant, wild with fury.

When he'd finished, Hammond expected Carr would shout back. Hammond knew he had just kissed his future goodbye with that outburst. His career was over. If he was lucky, he would be discharged. More likely, though, he was looking at a court martial. You simply didn't talk to a senior officer the way he just had. Chances were Hammond was going to spend some time in an army jail.

Major Carr opened his mouth to speak.

And then he froze.

And then he toppled over backwards.

He lay stiff on the floor. His eyes rolled up till only the whites showed. A rattle escaped his throat.

Hammond gazed down at Carr for nearly a minute.

That was how long it took for the truth to sink in. Major Carr was dead.

Chapter 17

Scorched Earth

The Chinook hurtled across dark seas. Storm-force winds buffeted the helicopter. Inside the cabin, everything shook and rattled. The Dead Brigade bounced in their cots.

Hammond was strapped into his seat, clutching the arm-rests hard. At the outset there had been talk of calling off the mission. The weather was vile and there was little chance of it improving in the next few hours.

But time was the most important thing. A group of militant eco-warriors called Scorched Earth had kidnapped the teenage daughter of the prime minister. They had snatched her from her boarding school and were holding her in a castle on an island off the east coast of Scotland. Scorched Earth would kill the girl unless the prime minister did as they asked. They wanted him to shut down every power station in the UK, at once. The coal-fired power stations, the gas-fired ones, the nuclear ones, all of them. Now. It was the only way, they said, to save the planet. And, also, the only way the prime minister could save his daughter.

Scorched Earth had cut off one of the girl's fingers and sent it to 10 Downing Street. Just to show they meant business.

They would cut off her head at midnight, if the prime minister didn't agree to their demands by then.

So, the Dead Brigade had been called in. They would be the first line of attack. If they failed, an SAS unit was standing by as back-up. The army was taking no chances with the life of the PM's daughter.

The castle was an old medieval fortress. It was made of solid stone, with small slits for windows. Scorched Earth had Gatling GAU-17 heavy machine guns, mounted on tripods. They had rocket launchers. They had grenades. They were armed to the teeth and willing to die for their cause.

To protect themselves further, they'd put landmines all around the castle. Only a madman would risk a full frontal assault on the place.

Only a madman, or a dead man.

Hammond looked at his troops as they were charged up, being prepared for yet another battle.

There were eleven of them now, not ten.

A new member had joined their ranks just two weeks ago.

He was fat and awkward. He wasn't the fastest mover among them. Even Slowcoach could outpace him.

His blubbery flesh wobbled as the Chinook battered through the storm.

Hammond hadn't yet come up with a nickname for this new recruit. But then, the new recruit didn't need one. He was someone whose name Hammond already knew.

Major Carr had died of a sudden, massive heart attack. It had happened right before Hammond's very eyes. A blood clot broke loose in one of Carr's arteries, entered his heart, and stopped it cold.

Hammond knew first aid. Once he had got over the first shock, he knelt down and tried to revive Carr using mouth-to-mouth breathing. It was no good. Hammond had then raised the alarm. Carr was taken swiftly by ambulance to the nearest hospital. But there was nothing they could do for him there. Carr was DOA, Dead On Arrival.

Later that same day, Hammond told Professor Lessing just what had happened. He described how he'd yelled at Carr and Carr had then collapsed. Hammond felt like he was confessing to a crime.

"It wasn't your fault, Dex," Professor Lessing told him. "Carr was a fat pig. This sort of thing happens to people like him all the time. Too many rich meals, not enough exercise. He was a heart attack waiting to happen."

"But if I hadn't let loose at him like that ..."

"It wasn't your fault," Professor Lessing said again. "How can I get that into your thick skull? Don't go beating yourself up over it. I know that's what you like to do. You're the sort of person who takes everything on himself. You have too much guilt about things. Just let go of it, Dex. Let go."

Good advice.

But Hammond was unable to follow it. At least, not all of it.

The Chinook's co-pilot came down from the cockpit into the cabin.

"Five minutes to drop-off," he said to Hammond. "The island's in sight."

Night and the storm provided cover. The Chinook hovered over the raging sea while an inflatable boat was dropped out of the back.

Hammond and his Dead Brigade paddled their way towards the island. The boat lurched and pitched in a sickening way.

They hit the island's one and only beach, a thin strip of pebbles within a shallow bay.

Hammond tied up the boat to a rock. The Dead Brigade moved up the shore to the foot of a cliff. The cliff sloped at an angle. It was a tough climb, but Hammond and his eleven men made it to the top.

The castle loomed against the wind-torn sky. Hammond spotted one of the Gatling gun emplacements, at the top of a tower.

Between the Dead Brigade and the castle there was an expanse of rough grass. Intelligence reports said that this was one of the areas where Scorched Earth had planted mines.

The sensible way to get to the castle was to go around the minefield. There was a rocky ridge on one side that led to the castle's north-west corner. That ought to be the Dead Brigade's route of attack. It was the way the SAS unit would go, if they were needed to go in and rescue the PM's daughter. No, *when* they were needed.

Hammond winced as the rain lashed his face. The same rain hurled itself into the faces of his troops, and they took no notice at all. It spattered against their cold skin. They felt nothing.

The eleven dead men stood ready, waiting for Hammond's orders.

Chief. Slowcoach. Niner. Earring. All of them.

Not forgetting Major Carr, of course.

Once again, a picture appeared in Hammond's head. In his mind's eye he saw souls in cages, prisoners screaming. He could free them.

He also saw soldiers in the Zagros mountains screaming in his dreams. He could free them too.

Project Osiris would go on, with or without him. Hammond knew that. Whatever happened, Professor Lessing would carry on with her work. She was a scientist. That was what she did. The work was everything to her. She would continue to raise the dead. Her moral conscience might tell her not to, but she could ignore it. If she drank enough brandy, she could ignore anything.

The rain poured down the dead soldiers' faces, like rivers of tears.

Hammond gave the order.

"Let's go," he said softly, pointing to the castle.

The Dead Brigade marched forward into the minefield.

The earth exploded under their feet. Mangling their bodies. Blowing off limbs.

They kept going. The ones that could still walk, walked. The ones who'd lost their legs crawled, pulling themselves along with their arms.

From the castle tower, the Gatling gun started to chatter. Tracer rounds shot through the sky, threads of light in the dark. The bullets smacked into dead flesh. The dead danced.

More mines went off. Still the Dead Brigade kept going forward across the killing ground.

The dead men's mouths were pulled into strange grim smiles, as one by one they were destroyed beyond repair.

And Warrant Officer Dex Hammond marched with them.

Want *more?*

Kill Clock

by

Allan Guthrie

Pearce's ex-girlfriend is back.

She needs twenty grand before midnight. Or she's dead.

She doesn't have the money. Nor does Pearce.

And time's running out. *Fast.*